OLE KÖNNECKE

YOU CAN DO IT, BERT!

GECKO PRESS

This is Bert.
It's his big day.

Bert is well prepared,
mentally and physically.

Bert checks everything
one more time.

A-ha! Bert's taking a running start.

No, he's not.

Come on, Bert.

Bert?

BERT!

Help.

Splash.

I did it!

When Bert says
he'll do something,
he does it.

That's our Bert.

This edition first published in 2014 by Gecko Press
PO Box 9335, Marion Square, Wellington 6141, New Zealand
info@geckopress.com

English language edition © Gecko Press Ltd 2014

First American edition published in 2015 by Gecko Press USA, an imprint of Gecko
Press Ltd. A catalog record for this book is available from the US Library of Congress.

Distributed in the United States and Canada by Lerner Publishing Group,
www.lernerbooks.com

Distributed in the United Kingdom by Bounce Sales and Marketing,
www.bouncemarketing.co.uk

Distributed in Australia by Scholastic Australia,
www.scholastic.com.au

Distributed in New Zealand by Random House NZ,
www.randomhouse.co.nz

A catalogue record for this book is available from the
National Library of New Zealand.

Original title: Du schaffst das!
By Ole Könnecke
© 2007, Ole Könnecke
© 2007, Sanssouci, Carl Hanser Verlag, Munich

Translated by Catherine Chidgey
Typesetting by Vida & Luke Kelly, New Zealand
Printed in China by Everbest Printing Co Ltd,
an accredited ISO 14001 & FSC certified printer

ISBN hardback 978-1-927271-03-2
ISBN paperback 978-1-927271-43-8

For more curiously good books, visit www.geckopress.com